KENNETH GRAHAME'S

THE WIND IN THE
WILLOWS

A GRAPHIC NOVEL

BY STEPHANIE PETERS
& FERN CANO

RAINTREE BOOKS
A CAPSTONE IMPRINT

Raintree is an imprint of Capstone Global Library
Limited, a company incorporated in England and Wales
having its registered office at 264 Banbury Road, Oxford,
OX2 7DY – Registered company number: 6695582

www.raintree.co.uk
myorders@raintree.co.uk

Designer: Kyle Grenz

ISBN 978-1-4747-2606-1 (paperback)
20 19 18 17
10 9 8 7 6 5 4 3 2 1

British Library Cataloguing in Publication Data
A full catalogue record for this book is available from the
British Library.

Every effort has been made to contact copyright holders
of material reproduced in this book. Any omissions
will be rectified in subsequent printings if notice is given
to the publisher.

Printed and bound in China.

CONTENTS

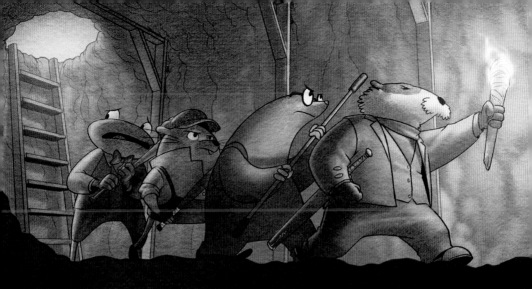

ALL ABOUT *THE WIND IN THE WILLOWS*

Author Kenneth Grahame first created his beloved characters Toad, Mole, Ratty and Badger for his son, Alastair. The animals' grand adventures were bedtime stories for the boy, and when Grahame travelled he would expand upon the stories in letters to his son.

Grahame retired from a position with the Bank of England in 1908. He and his family moved to live on the River Thames, which became the inspiration for the setting of *The Wind in the Willows*. With characters and setting in place, Grahame completed the manuscript for his children's book. It was published that year, in the heart of what has been called the "Golden Age of Children's Literature."

However, the critics were not kind, and, in general, gave the book poor reviews. But it didn't matter: the public loved the stories and the lessons they taught. One of the book's biggest fans was US President Theodore Roosevelt. He wrote to Grahame, saying that he had "read it and reread it, and had come to accept the characters as old friends." When Roosevelt visited England in 1910, he requested to meet Grahame in person.

The play *Toad of Toad Hall* by famed Winnie-the-Pooh author A.A. Milne brought Toad's adventures to the stage in 1929. It is just one of dozens of creative works inspired by the four friends of the Thames Valley.

MR TOAD

13

But Mr Toad didn't care one bit. He'd fallen in love…

TOOT
TOOT

…with motor cars.

And again.

And again.

What should we do?

Wait for Badger to talk sense into Mr Toad.

Mole got tired of waiting for Badger to show up.

He went into the Wild Wood to find Badger himself.

Rat had warned him about the Wild Wood…

Stay out! It's extremely dangerous!

WILD WOOD

Mole went in anyway.

Badger gave them a warm welcome.

Rat told Badger about Mr Toad.

Seven cars. Seven crashes.

It's been awful.

They ate while Badger thought things over.

When the weather turns warm, I'll talk to Mr Toad.

Thank you, Badger.

The friends slept well.

It led to the river. And Mole's old home.

Why, I used to live here!

Where is your home?

That way.

Mole's home wasn't as spacious as Badger's, or as grand as Mr Toad's, or as airy as Rat's.

But it's mine.

MOLE'S END

Thank you for welcoming me, Mole-y.

Still, Mole didn't plan to stay long.

I like my new adventurous life!

Me too.

They spent the first half of winter at Mole's home…

CHAPTER 3

MR TOAD'S FOLLY

...and the second half of winter at Rat's home.

When warmer weather finally returned...

KNOCK KNOCK KNOCK

Badger! Good to see you!

Sadly, I bring bad news...

...Mr Toad has purchased a powerful new car.

Oh, no. We must stop him –

– Before it's too late!

Agreed.

The friends immediately set out for Mr Toad's home.

As soon as they arrived…

While Toad languished in prison, Rat, Mole, and the others got on with their lives.

There were terrible moments.

My son is missing!

Don't worry, we'll find him!

And wonderful moments.

There he is!

My boy!

Ahhh!

It fits!

How do I look?

Just like her!

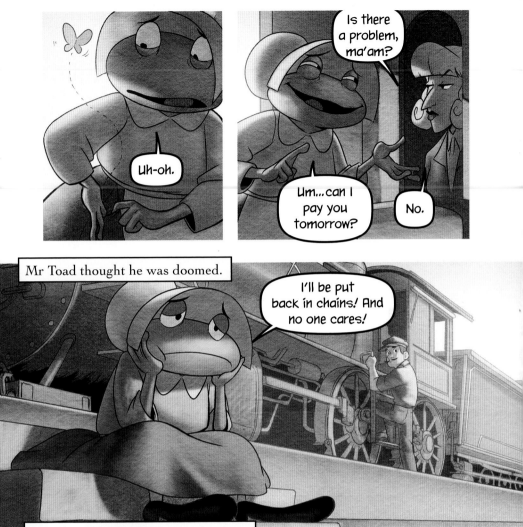

The policemen passed by without seeing him.

Ha-ha! You'll never catch me!

But his troubles were far from over.

Which way is home?

It was a long, cold night.

Mr Toad swam for shore.

Horrid, nasty, crawly toad!

The joke is on her! I don't need her barge.

NEIGH?

Ha, ha! I'm so clever!

The swim cleaned his disguise. Soon, the hot sunshine had dried it.

Much better.

The sun also made him sleepy.

Snore! Snore!

SIGH.

A delicious smell soon woke him.

Food?

Mr Toad followed the smell.

Something stopped him.

It's a car!

He flagged them down, hoping for a ride.

He was overjoyed when it stopped –

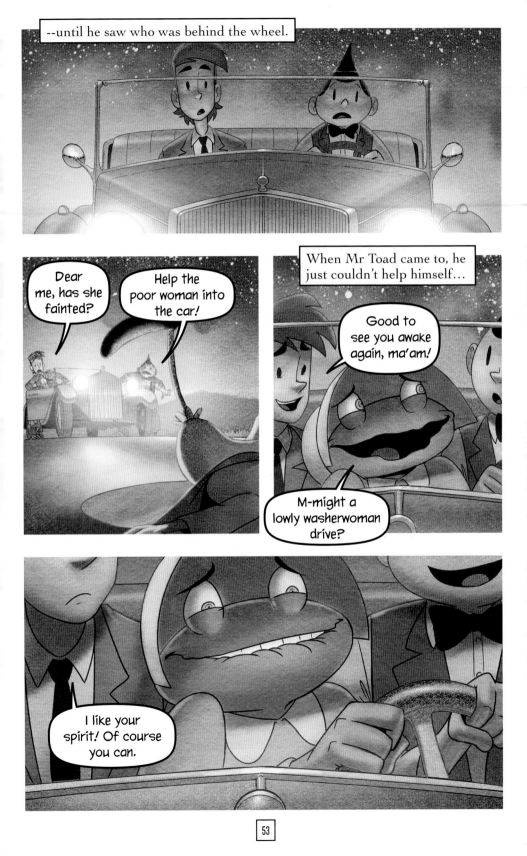

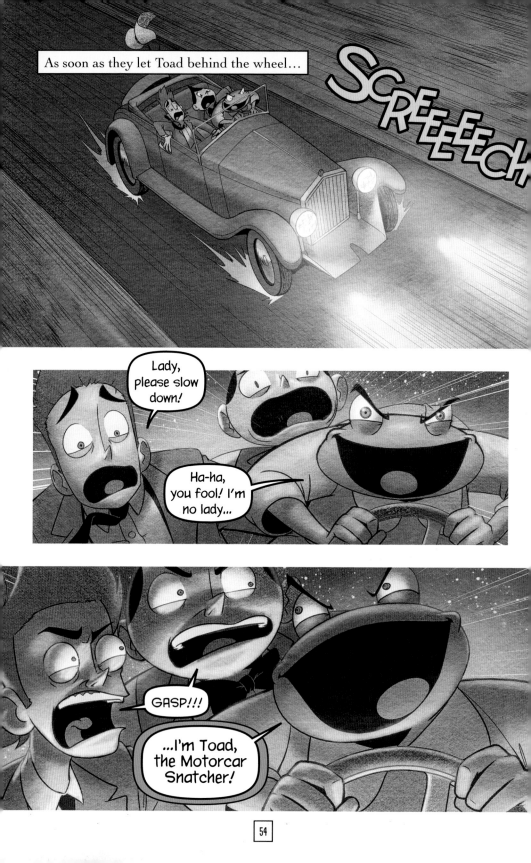

"And the stoats came in through a window!"

"Mole and Badger were taken completely by surprise!"

"They were lucky to escape with their lives…"

…The Wild Wooders own it now, Toady.

Do they now? I'll see about that!

Mr Toad set off for Toad Hall at once.

BANG

He didn't stay long.

But he didn't give up, either.

I'll sneak into my boat-house.

Wicked animals!

It'll be your head next time!

But Mr Toad surprised them all.

Actually...

...Badger was the mastermind. And Mole and Rat did most of the fighting.

And from that time on, the friends were hailed as heroes by all.

The End.

ABOUT THE RETELLING AUTHOR AND ILLUSTRATOR

After more than 10 years working as a children's book editor, **Stephanie True Peters** started writing books herself. She has written 40 books, including the New York Times best seller *A Princess Primer: A Fairy Godmother's Guide to Being a Princess.* When not at her computer, Peters enjoys playing with her two children, exercising at the gym or working on home improvement projects with her patient and supportive husband, Daniel.

Fernando Cano is an emerging illustrator born in Mexico City, Mexico. He currently resides in Monterrey, Mexico, where he works as a full-time illustrator and colourist at Graphikslava studio. He has done illustration work for Marvel, DC Comics and role-playing games like *Pathfinder* from Paizo Publishing. In his spare time, he enjoys spending time with friends, singing, rowing and drawing.

GLOSSARY

barge large, flat boat used to transport goods

brawn muscular strength

canal waterway or channel dug across land so that boats can travel between two bodies of water

horrid very unpleasant

languish become weak

luxury something that is not needed but adds great ease and comfort

sentence time spent in prison or a correctional facility as punishment for a crime

spacious larger than average in size or capacity

stoat small mammal that is part of the weasel family

trappings ornamental covering for horses

COMPREHENSION QUESTIONS
READING QUESTIONS

1. What is Mr Toad like at the beginning of the story? How does he change? Does he learn anything by the end of the story?

2. The settings in this graphic novel are detailed and well illustrated. Describe what each of the main characters' homes looks like on both the inside and outside. How do the homes of Mole, Mr Toad and Badger reflect their personalities?

3. Why do Mr Toad's friends guard his door and not allow him to come out? Why does Mr Toad escape from his friends' watch?

COMPREHENSION QUESTIONS
WRITING PROMPTS

1. Do you think Mr Toad is a good friend? Would you want to be his friend? Why or why not?

2. Imagine you are Mole, Ratty or Badger. Write a diary entry in which you describe how Mr Toad's actions make you feel.

3. Look closely at the illustrations in this graphic novel, focusing on the setting and scenery of the river and the surrounding land. On a piece of paper, write a vivid and colourful description of the river valley based on details you see in the illustrations.

READ THEM ALL!

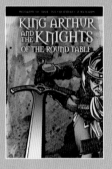

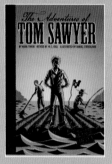

CHARLES DICKENS'S
A CHRISTMAS CAROL
A GRAPHIC NOVEL

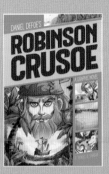

DANIEL DEFOE'S
ROBINSON CRUSOE
A GRAPHIC NOVEL

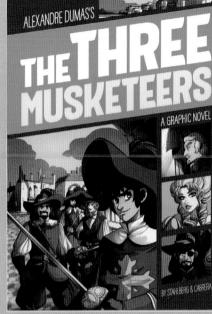

ALEXANDRE DUMAS'S
THE THREE MUSKETEERS
A GRAPHIC NOVEL
BY STAHLBERG & CABRERA

JULES VERNE'S
AROUND THE WORLD IN 80 DAYS
A GRAPHIC NOVEL
BY KORNAY & INER

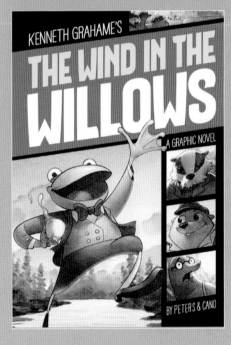

KENNETH GRAHAME'S
THE WIND IN THE WILLOWS
A GRAPHIC NOVEL
BY PETERS & CANO

LEWIS CARROLL'S
ALICE IN WONDERLAND
A GRAPHIC NOVEL
BY POWELL & FERRAN

J.M. BARRIE'S
PETER PAN
A GRAPHIC NOVEL
BY MEDINA & CANO